THIS CANDLEWICK BOOK BELONGS TO:

*To Pete, Caitlin,*
*and the Mighty Huffer*

First U.S. paperback edition 2003

The Library of Congress has cataloged the hardcover edition as follows:

Graham, Bob, date.
Benny : an adventure story / Bob Graham. — 1st U.S. ed.
p.    cm.
Summary: When Benny the dog steals the show from Brillo the magician, he is forced to look for a new home where his rare talents such as juggling and tap dancing will be appreciated.
ISBN 0-7636-0813-0 (hardcover)
[1. Dogs—Fiction. 2. Magicians—Fiction.]  I. Title.
PZ7.G751667Be    1999
[E]—dc21       98-029210

ISBN 0-7636-1703-2 (paperback)

10 9 8 7 6 5 4 3 2 1

Printed in Hong Kong

This book was typeset in Garamond Book Educational.
The illustrations were done in watercolor and ink.

Candlewick Press
2067 Massachusetts Avenue
Cambridge, Massachusetts 02140

visit us at www.candlewick.com

# Benny
## An Adventure Story

Bob Graham

CANDLEWICK PRESS
CAMBRIDGE, MASSACHUSETTS

**Benny** had skills
that were rare in a dog.
As an assistant to Brillo
the Magician, he did his
job well enough . . .
But Benny had talents
all of his own.
He could juggle three
clubs at once and throw
a rope like a cowboy.

He could escape from the Houdini Deathtrap while playing the harmonica. "Bravo!" cried the audience.

His tap dancing met with thunderous applause, and how the dust rose from those well-trodden boards!

Brillo muttered darkly under his moustache.

Benny was becoming more popular than he was.

"OUT! and never come back!" cried Brillo.

Benny's bottom lip quivered with emotion as he left the stage forever.

He spent his last coins on a can of dog food and a can opener.

In a bleak railroad yard he ate
the last of his lamb chunks and pasta.
He wiped his mouth on his spotted scarf, and then . . .

Benny jumped aboard
a moving freight train.

To the rhythm of the wheels,
he tapped his foot and sang,

"Oh, blue is me!
Oh, dearie me,
I'm as down as
a dog can be."

And while he slept, the train
continued its rhythm:

OUT, OUT . . . .
and never come back.
OUT, OUT . . . .
and never come back.

Benny woke the next morning to the smell of fresh-cut grass and countryside.

He put his harmonica in his bag and leapt off the train. "I will bring my tricks to the world," he said.

But the world did not want Benny's tricks. Nobody wanted a dancing sheepdog.

Nobody wanted a tiny rope-throwing cattle dog.

Nobody wanted a plate-juggling kitchen dog.

Nobody wanted
a guard dog
who played
the harmonica.

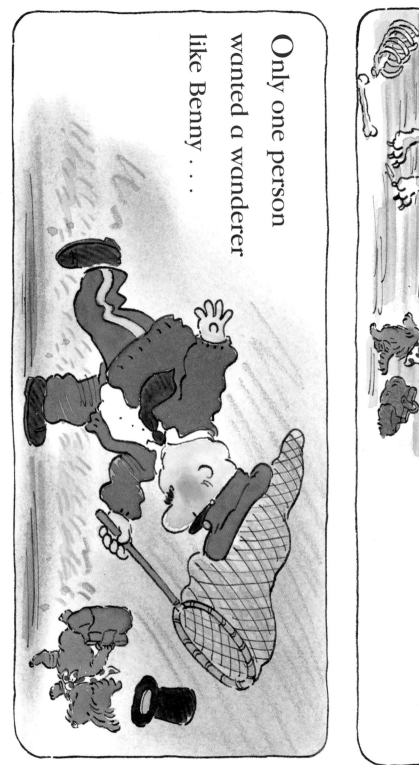

Only one person
wanted a wanderer
like Benny . . .

but Benny did
not want HIM!

"I will find myself a home," he said and set off in search of one.

He sat above the roaring engines of mighty road trucks.

He crossed rivers

and deserts.

He stood on
mountains and
moaned at
the moon.

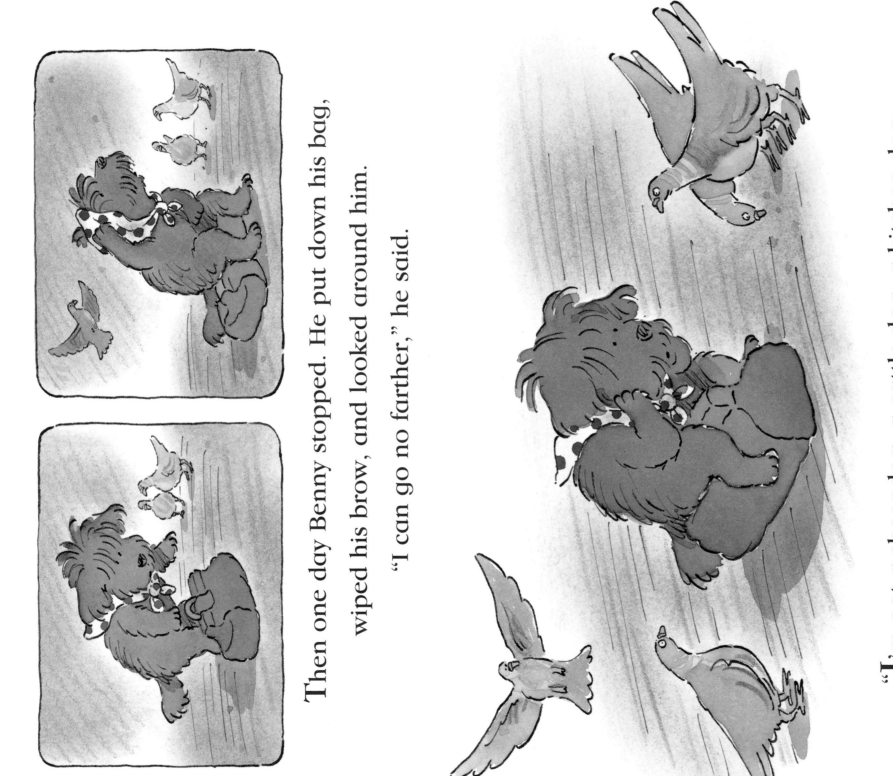

Then one day Benny stopped. He put down his bag, wiped his brow, and looked around him.

"I can go no farther," he said.

"I'm not a sheepdog, a cattle dog, a kitchen dog or a guard dog. So what sort of dog am I?"

"I am Benny!
And I will do
what I do.
And this time,
the world shall
come to me."

Benny's feet beat out the rhythm of the train on the tracks,

and his harmonica howled like the desert wind and

pulsed like the engines of the mighty road trucks.

Many coins rattled into Benny's cup that day, and many faces passed by. Then someone stood in front of him. His breath stopped. His feet stopped. The sun came out.

It was Mary Kelly.

and her brother,

and her grandad,

and her father,

And Mary's mother,

and her grandma,

and her baby sister, Morag.

For Benny, and the Kellys too,
it was love at first sight.
Off he went, the coins heavy in his cup.
At last, he had found a place to call home.

Now, each night after
dinner, the music starts,
and each night the
floorboards shake.
Mary's and Benny's feet
beat to the rhythm of
the jigs and the reels.

And Benny lives up there,
on the hill, to this day.

Bob Graham says Benny is based on the life of one of his own dogs. "We got him from a shelter, a victim of a broken home, we were told. And he told me the rest one day when he was sitting on a pillow in my workroom. So it's all true!"